Shoo Rayner

Shoo began his career as an illustrator in a garden shed near Machynlleth. He drew for Michael Morpurgo and Rose Impey, but people kept encouraging him to write. Many years and more than 175 books later, Shoo has built a worldwide following for his award-winning how-to-draw videos on YouTube. http://www.shoorayner.com/

Shoo lives in the Forest of Dean with his wife and three cats.

Shoo's first book about Harri and Tân, *Dragon Gold*, was highly commended by the Tir na n'Og award 2015.

To Helena Cochrane – the CEO

Also in this series,

available from Firefly Press:

Dragon Gold

Dragon White

Dragon Red

First published in 2017
by Firefly Press
25 Gabalfa Road, Llandaff North, Cardiff, CF14 2JJ
www.fireflypress.co.uk

A CIP catalogue record of this book is available from the British Library.

ISBN 9781910080481
ebook ISBN 9781910080498

This book has been published with the support of the Welsh Books Council.

Typeset by Elaine Sharples
Printed by Pulsio

Dragon Red

Shoo Rayner

Chapter One

The tall tower loomed over the town. At its foot, the hooded figure of a man pressed back into the dark shadows. He waited a moment, to make sure he'd not been seen.

There were no security cameras watching that part of the castle, as no one would would be stupid enough to do what he was about to try. Slowly, hand over hand, inch by inch, fingers tightly gripping the sharp granite blocks, he scaled the fortress walls.

A short while later, he appeared on top of the battlements, raised his arms, punched the air and let out a wild cry of triumph.

As the sound faded, another shape overshadowed him. Huge wings unfurled against the bright, moonlit sky. The unmistakable silhouette of a dragon! It opened its mouth wide, roaring jets of

red and yellow flame into the night. The man's face glowed in the blazing light. A smile spread across his face.

The man climbed up awkwardly onto the dragon's back. As one, the dragon and its master swooped over the rooftops, blazing fire and leaving a trail of gleeful laughter in their wake. Curtained bedroom windows lit up, as the townsfolk were woken from their peaceful dreams.

An alarm sounded. Sirens wailed in the distance. A loud, electronic voice broke into Harri's dream.

'This is a police emergency announcement. All residents must stay indoors. Do not leave your house for any reason. I repeat, stay indoors. A dragon has escaped. If you see it, report it at once. Under no circumstances should you approach it yourself.'

'Wake up, Harri! The police are here. They want

to talk to you.' Harri's mum gently shook her son awake.

Harri threw the covers off and sat up in bed, blinking and shaking the sleep out of his eyes. He felt confused and muzzy. He'd been dreaming of the dragons. Was this still the dream?

'What's that noise?' he croaked.

'They've set off the old air raid sirens,' Mum explained.

'Why? What's happened?'

'It's Ryan's dad,' said Mum. 'He's managed to free his dragon from the tower. No one knows where they've gone. The police are downstairs. They want to talk to you.'

He wasn't quite sure if he was really awake or still dreaming. He put his dressing gown on and followed his mum downstairs. 'But I don't know anything about it,' he grumbled. 'I haven't seen Ryan's dad for weeks.' Ryan and Harri were good friends and in the same class at school.

Imelda, Harri's sort of adopted granny, put a mug of tea on the kitchen table in front of him.

'It's serious,' she said. 'This is the Chief Constable. And this is Detective Chief Inspector Griffiths and Detective Sergeant Hughes. They want to ask you some questions.'

Chapter Two

The Chief Constable introduced himself and soon left to hold a news conference, but the two detectives stayed for what seemed like hours, asking the same questions, checking every detail of how Harri and Ryan's dad both came to own dragons.

'So tell us again how you got Tân,' DS Hughes asked, patiently noting down everything Harri said in her little black book.

Harri glanced at Imelda. You could barely notice the movement of her head, but Harri knew what she meant: 'Don't tell them the whole truth. They won't understand.'

'I was playing up on the hills and I found an egg,' he lied. Harri felt his cheeks burning with embarrassment. He was sure they knew he was

lying, but he had practised his cover story well. 'I brought it home and it hatched into Tân — my dragon. He was so cute and helpless, I kept him and looked after him.'

Harri avoided looking in their eyes. He felt like a criminal. Would they arrest him for not telling the truth?

'Have you any idea how Ryan's dad got his dragon?' asked DCI Griffiths. 'You and Ryan are good friends, aren't you?'

'Yes.' Harri shrugged. 'He must have found an egg too.' The truth was even more unbelievable. If he told them, they really would think he was lying.

Mum had a shop called Merlin's Cave where she sold magical things like dreamcatchers and crystals. She also sold tourist stuff and bottled holy water from St Gertrude's Well.

Since Imelda had come to live with them, business had improved a lot. Imelda was a witch.

Not a kid's-book type of witch, but one who knew the old ways and how to mix plants and flowers that she harvested from the fields and hedgerows. Now they sold her spells and love potions in the shop. Customers loved them.

When they first met, Harri had told Imelda about his school's Eisteddfod challenge. There had been a prize of dragon gold for anyone who could make a dragon fly for more than ten seconds. She had wanted to help him. She crumpled up his dragon drawing and placed it inside a magic egg.

A week later the egg cracked open and Tân came into their lives — bright red, cute and perky and with a huge appetite for worms and chocolate. They could never have guessed how much trouble owning a dragon would turn out to be.

Harri and Ryan were friends in school. But Ryan's dad liked winning. He liked to make sure his son Ryan won everything. On the day of the challenge, his radio-controlled model of a Chinese J-20

Mighty Dragon Stealth Fighter Aircraft and Harri's Tân came equal first.

That wasn't good enough for Ryan's dad. Beating Harri became a burning obsession. He blackmailed Imelda and made her turn his own drawing of a fierce white dragon, Draca, into the real thing.

The two dragons finally met at the Ancient Briton's Re-enactment Society bank-holiday display, frightening the crowd when Draca attacked Tân. They were captured and taken into police custody.

Thanks to ancient laws that Harri and Imelda managed to discover in time, the dragon's lives were spared. They were allowed to live, as long as they were always locked within the walls of Castle Gertrude.

But now one of them had escaped. The law could no longer protect it. The creature was a menace and a danger to human life.

Chapter Three

DS Hughes' phone rang. 'They've caught Ryan's dad forty miles away,' she explained. 'He was walking along the side of a busy dual carriageway, but there was no sign of the dragon. He's at the police station drinking tea and eating chocolate biscuits, but he's saying nothing.'

'We'll go and interview him now,' said DCI Griffiths. 'If we can't get any sense out of him, we'll have to let him go. We can't prove he's broken any laws, so we've got no real reason to charge him.'

As they got up to leave, Harri had a moment of panic. 'I'm going to be late for school!'

'School's closed today,' said DS Hughes. 'We don't want dragons attacking the playground, so you've got the day off.' She pulled a card out of her wallet and handed it to Harri. 'That's my phone number.

If you get any ideas, remember anything or need help, call me any time, day or night.' She looked into Harri's eyes. 'Promise?'

'I promise,' said Harri. He put the card into his back pocket and closed and locked the door behind the officers. The bell tinkled gently.

'Those blooming dragons!' Mum sighed. 'They've been nothing but trouble.'

'Not Tân!' Harri and Imelda complained, as one.

Mum folded her arms and frowned at them. This was all their fault, creating dragons with magic eggs! 'I'm going to the cash and carry,' she said. 'I need to stock up on some things for the shop.'

Harri looked concerned. 'But the police say that we shouldn't…'

'Oh bother the police! If I can't open the shop, then I'm going out. I'm not sitting round here doing nothing all day!' She took her coat off the row of hooks in the passage, jangled her keys and slammed the door shut behind her. A moment

later her car drove down the side road and into the silent street.

Harri stared out of the shop door window and turned over the open sign so it read: 'Closed'.

Imelda busied herself in the kitchen. 'Tea and cake always helps,' she said, putting mugs and a plate of fruitcake on the table.

'Well!' she sighed, settling down in her comfy chair. 'This is all my fault.'

'It's all Ryan's dad's fault!' Harri said, crossly. 'He's the one who let Draca escape.'

'No,' Imelda smiled. 'It's all my fault for magicking the dragons in the first place. I was showing off when I made Tân out of your dragon drawing. I didn't really think about how hard it would be to keep a real dragon secret. I felt you were special the moment I met you and I wanted to please you.'

'Special? How do you mean, special?' Harri frowned.

'Oh! There I go again, stirring things up.' She looked awkward and changed the subject. 'I think you should go and see Tân. Check he's alright. You know what the police will do if he escapes as well.'

Tân. Of course he should go and see if Tân was alright.

Harri was allowed to visit his dragon in Castle Gertrude any time he liked. He went every day to clean Tân's lair with fresh straw, give him chocolate treats and to make sure he was being looked after properly. Tân would be wondering where he was and what was going on. Tân might be scared. Tân needed him now. But more importantly, and this was something Imelda understood, Harri needed Tân.

Chapter Four

'I don't understand you any more! Just get in the car and don't say a word!' Ryan's mum had finally lost her self-control and was pushing her husband into the passenger seat of her shiny, new Mercedes.

They'd asked her to come and collect him from the police station. She'd fumed all the way there, ignoring her son in the back. Now she drove home in a silent rage. As they pulled into their driveway, her anger exploded.

'You'd better get a grip on life or we are finished!' she hissed at her husband, spraying foamy spit into his face. 'You are losing your mind. You need to see a doctor. You and your flaming dragon! You're living in a fantasy world. Get real or get your stuff and move out — I can't stand it any more!'

Ryan watched his parents from the back seat. His stomach lurched with every harsh word his mother hurled at his dad. He'd never seen her like this before, nor his father, who sat motionless, wincing occasionally as the insults hit home.

She climbed out of the car, slammed the door and went into the house. Ryan sat in the expensive, white leather silence. His dad unclipped his seatbelt and turned round to face him.

'Sorry about that, son,' he smiled weakly. 'This is all my fault.'

'What are you going to do, Dad?' Ryan whispered.

'I am going to do what I have to do, son.' He nodded, as if he were agreeing with an invisible audience. Then he got out of the car and walked over to the garage.

Ryan sat and watched him pull up the roller-door and go inside. The car ticked as the engine cooled. A short while later his dad reappeared. He'd

changed. He must have had new clothes stashed away in the garage. Not normal clothes. He was wearing some serious, camouflage all-weather clothing and wore enormous hiking boots. A large backpack weighed him down as he marched off towards the gate.

Ryan fought to undo his seatbelt and flung open the door.

'Dad!' he shouted. 'Where are you going?'

'I am going to do what I have to do, son,' his dad called back. And with a wave he was gone.

Chapter Five

It felt a bit weird, walking through the deserted town. Harri felt suspicious eyes watching him from behind tightly shut windows. He imagined the frightened conversations going on behind the town's locked doors: 'There he goes! There's the boy who started all this dragon nonsense. It's all his fault.'

Harri had never meant any of it to happen. Sometimes, when he thought about his life since Tân had hatched, it seemed like he was living in a storybook. He knew dragons didn't really exist and yet … he had one! What would have happened if the court hadn't locked Tân up in the castle? Dragons keep growing. Harri couldn't have kept him a secret forever.

The town had no reason to complain. There were

queues to see the dragons every day. Tourists poured into St Gertrude's. The little town's cafes, shops and hotels were full to bursting. St Gertrude's had become 'The Dragon Town'. Shop windows and street signs were all covered in red and white dragons. Everyone was making money out of the two creatures in one way or another. Harri didn't know why his mum was so cross — the shop had never been so busy. They sold loads of dragon souvenirs to the tourists who wanted to see the very place where the first dragon had been born and maybe meet Harri — The Dragon Boy!

But today the castle gates were closed to the public. A policeman stood guard outside.

'I'm just going in to check on my dragon,' Harri called. The policeman nodded. Harri was a celebrity here. Everyone knew one of the dragons was his. But no one really understood. Only he and Ryan's dad knew what it felt like – no one else could understand the bond between a dragon and its master.

Harri slipped his security keycard into the reader on the side door of the gift shop and let himself in. He came this way every day, but the castle had never been so deserted before. It was eerily quiet.

He climbed the ancient stone spiral staircase up to where the dragons lived. The heavy ironwork door that had held Draca, the white dragon, in captivity, hung open and useless. The display on the electronic keypad in the lock flashed the word 'error' in red, insistent letters. How had Ryan's dad done it? How had he climbed in and released Draca … and why? It was all going to end in tears. Draca would never be allowed to come back here alive.

Harri walked warily around the corner. 'No!' he gasped.

The door to Tân's lair stood wide open, the lock flashing 'error' too. The cage was empty. Oh no! Had Tân flown away with Draca and Ryan's dad?

A sound made him jump. A clicking noise … like dragon claws on a stone floor?

'Tân?' Harri called into the gloomy, unlit corridor.

He heard an excited snort from the darkness at the end of the corridor as Tân heard his voice — but he heard something else too… A voice in his head!

As he looked down the corridor and Tân's eyes met his, the voice in his head rang clear as a bell.

'Harri!'

'Tân!'

Harri could hear Tân's voice and knew it as if he'd heard it all his life.

'Tân! I can hear you!'

Tân's face crumpled into a smile — a human smile! No, it wasn't that. It was a dragon smile. But now Harri could read Tân's expressions as if he were a dragon too. Something had brought them closer together than ever before.

'What happened last night?' Harri asked.

'Ryan's dad came for Draca. They stood where you are now, laughing at me, daring me to escape

with them and to help them find Merlin's gold. When I refused,' Tân continued, 'Draca said that next time we meet, it will be a fight to the death.'

Harri shuddered. If Tân died, a part of him would die too.

'Draca has grown so big!' said Tân. 'Dragons can choose to feed on bitterness and greed. It depends who made them and why. Draca is full of hatred. He wants revenge on those who locked him up and now he want's Merlin's gold too. His master has changed as well … his will has left him. His heart is not strong like yours. Draca is the master now and Ryan's dad does what he tells him to do.'

There was something different about Tân. He looked grown up in a dragon sort of way. Harri hadn't realised quite how big Tân had grown. The castle lair was beginning to look a bit small for his handsome beast.

A voice from the police loudspeakers boomed through the small, slit windows. 'The Emergency is

over. You may come out of your homes. If you see a white dragon, report its whereabouts to the police immediately. Thank you!'

'What are we going to do?' Harri asked.

'I don't know,' said Tân. 'When the time comes, we'll do what we have to do, but now I think you should talk to Imelda. If Draca is after Merlin's treasure, then she will know all about it. She knows about the old ways.'

Harri brought new straw and food. He tidied up Tân's cage and locked him back inside. He didn't want Tân to suffer what lay ahead for Draca. Tân hadn't done anything wrong.

Anyone watching would have seen a boy quietly going about his work. All the conversations between the two were secret in Harri's head.

Chapter Six

No one saw Ryan's dad climb the stile over the fence and leave the street and the world of civilisation behind.

The ancient footpath was like a tunnel through the trees. No one could see him, or know where to follow him. He had a new phone with an unregistered number in his bag, so no one could track his signal. He'd switch it on when he was ready.

The footpath opened out into the wild, open country in the hills above St Gertrude's. A couple of dog walkers came by, but they never noticed the man in camouflage gear, hunkered down in the bracken, waiting patiently, deadly still, until they had gone past and on their way.

One of them came within a metre of him and never suspected.

Ryan's dad smiled to himself. 'I'm good at this!' he thought.

Soon he was in the wilderness. No one ever came here but sheep and the occasional farmer. He took out his map and compass and plotted a route across the wild, lonely mountain passes.

He checked his watch. 6:15 PM 29 April.

'Not long till the Eve of May Day,' he told a family of startled rabbits, as he heaved on his backpack and headed west, into the pinky, golden sky of a warm, spring sunset.

Chapter Seven

'How was Tân?' Imelda asked.

'Okay. Is Mum back?'

Imelda shook her head. 'Was Tân alright? Was he okay? Was he different?'

'Different? What do you mean, different?'

She knew. Imelda knew something!

Imelda let the silence hang, growing longer and wider until Harri couldn't bear it any more.

'Tân was talking to me!' he gushed. 'In my head! Like either he can think in English or I can think in Dragon.'

Imelda nodded. 'It feels like the old prophecies are coming true, but when I say that, it makes me sound like a silly old woman.'

'What do you mean?' Harri was confused. Everything that had seemed safe and certain

yesterday had changed. He felt as though the ground was moving under his feet — his world was tearing apart, out of his control. 'I don't understand. I—I kind of… sort of… I sort of *feel* different too!'

He blew out his cheeks and stared at Imelda, waiting to see if she had an explanation.

'You know the story of the red and white dragon in the *Mabinogion*, don't you?' Imelda asked.

Harri rolled his eyes. 'Yeah! Mr Davies is always going on about it in school. How King Lludd captured the red and white dragons and buried them at Dinas Emrys. He'd told us that story just before you came into the shop for the first time. That's why I was drawing a dragon that day.'

'And that is why Tân is like he is,' said Imelda. 'Because you were drawing the Red Dragon from the stories in the *Mabinogion*, so that is what Tân is made of — he is the Red Dragon. His destiny lies at Dinas Emrys, Merlin's Castle, where Merlin hid his treasure.'

'Mum and I went to Dinas Emrys just before Tân hatched out of his egg.'

'I know … I saw you there,' said Imelda.

Harri looked shocked. 'Were you spying on us?'

Imelda smiled and shook her head. 'No, I was at a place called the Grove of the Magicians nearby, looking for some rare herbs that grow there.'

'And you saw us?'

'Yes!'

Imelda began to tell the tale of Merlin and the dragons. Her voice was hypnotic, weaving pictures in Harri's head — not dreams, but images that seemed to be long lost memories of a distant past.

'King Vortigern needed to build a fortress and Dinas Emrys was the perfect place — a rocky hill with good views down the valley, from where you could keep a watch for Saxon invaders.

'But every night, the ground would shake and rumble, bringing down the newly built fortress walls. The king's wise men said the only solution

was to sprinkle the ground with the blood of a fatherless child. Merlin was the right child at the right time in the right place. He was the child they chose.'

Harri shivered at the thought. 'They didn't kill a boy, did they?'

'No,' Imelda smiled. 'Nothing bad happened to him. Merlin was well chosen, for he knew the old ways. He told King Vortigern that there was a chamber below the castle. King Lludd had locked two dragons in there and they fought each other every night. It was they who caused the ground to shake.

'Vortigern ordered a hole to be dug and Merlin was proved correct. But the dragons escaped and fought each other almost to the death. The white dragon fled and the red dragon came to live with St Gertrude, here in the castle where Tân lives now.'

'They finished building the fortress and named it Dinas Emrys — or Merlin's Castle. Emrys is the

old Welsh name for Merlin. They say that the chamber under the castle is still full of Merlin's gold and that one day a fatherless child will come to claim it. A bell will ring and the hillside will open for him.'

The hairs on Harri's neck stood up on end and his arms prickled with gooseflesh.

'I'm a fatherless child!' Harri whispered. 'I've never met my dad and we haven't heard from him for years. For all we know he could be dead.'

Imelda nodded slowly.

'Tân says that Draca wants that treasure,' Harri exclaimed. 'Do you think the story is true? That there's real treasure? Could I be that fatherless child?'

Imelda folded her arms and studied the boy's eager face closely. 'Who knows?' she said, mysteriously. 'What will be, will be.'

Chapter Eight

'So there you are!' Draca's voice growled inside Ryan's dad's head.

'I've got everything we need in my rucksack,' Ryan's dad explained. 'Are you hungry?'

Draca licked his lips. 'I've eaten!' his voice gurgled with dark pleasure. For the first time, Ryan's dad noticed the blood smeared across the dragon's face.

'Lamb is very tasty!' Draca chortled.

'They won't like you killing sheep,' said Ryan's dad. 'They'll come looking for us.'

'Let them! It doesn't matter to me,' Draca sneered. 'It's time for you to call and make that silly, little red dragon come and meet its fate. It's time to use him and put an end to him!'

Chapter Nine

Harri's mum bustled in through the back door carrying cardboard boxes full of stuff for the shop.

'Help me put these in the shop, will you, Harri?' she asked. 'We can sort them out later.'

As Harri stacked the boxes behind the counter, he heard a timid knock at the shop door.

'Ryan! What are you doing here?'

Warily, Ryan came into the shop, followed by his mum. Their two mothers had never really met properly. They were both full-time businesswomen and always busy. They nodded to each other politely.

'It's Dad,' said Ryan. 'He's gone off, dressed like he's going camping in the mountains. We don't know what to do. He's left his phone behind so we

can't call him. He's obviously going to meet up with Draca.'

Ryan and his mum stared at Harri. It was easy to see in their pale, worried faces the point of exhaustion that Ryan's dad had brought them to. He'd been behaving more and more strangely for weeks … ever since he'd first got his dragon and had been unwell with dragon fever. They hoped Harri or Imelda might have some answers.

The shop bell tinkled.

'Mr Davies!' Harri said, surprised. 'What are you doing here?

'It's all over the news!' Mr Davies gushed, breathlessly. 'How's Tân? Is he alright?'

As well as being Harri's school teacher, Mr Davies ran the Ancient Briton Re-enactment Society, the group of hairy, bearded men who met at weekends and dressed up to have battles with the Saxon Re-enactment Society.

Mr Davies was mad about ancient history and

dragons in particular. Tân was the Ancient Briton Re-enactment Society's mascot. They sponsored Tân's lair at the castle. Mr Davies felt that if Tân wasn't actually his, at least he had a sort of share of him.

'Draca, the white dragon, has been seen killing sheep up in the mountains,' he said, eyes wide and full of excitement. 'There's going to be serious trouble.'

The door tinkled again. Harri recognised the smiling face that appeared in the doorway, but couldn't think who it was.

'Hello, Harri! We're from the TV. We wondered if we could ask you a few questions on camera about your dragon?' The smiling lady smiled even more, showing off her expensive, brilliant white teeth. She was from the local TV News. That's where Harri knew her from.

'Go away!' Harri's mum waved her hands and shooed the woman out of the shop. 'We've nothing

to say. Harri is a minor and if you don't go away I'll call the police and get you arrested for harassing him!'

The TV presenter kept smiling, but she backed off and waited on the other side of the street, where she was joined by a growing throng of reporters, cameramen and passing busybodies.

'It's like Piccadilly Circus out there!' Harri's mum complained.

The bell tinkled again.

‘I said out and I mean out … oh!’ Harri’s mum turned to face the Chief Constable, who was barging through the front door, followed by DCI Griffiths and DS Hughes. Outside, lights flashed and TV people with microphones called questions with loud, insistent voices.

‘Sorry to disturb you,’ the Chief Constable said firmly but politely to everyone in the room. ‘We need to talk to Harri again.’

In the back room, away from the the prying eyes of the news reporters, it felt like a war counsel. The police were surprised but pleased to see Ryan and his mum were there too.

‘We were coming to see you next,’ said DS Hughes.

‘Ryan’s dad is now a fugitive from justice,’ said the Chief Constable. ‘He’s been seen up in the mountains with that white dragon of his. It’s been killing sheep. This can’t go on. Something will have to be done. I feel like calling in the army and shooting it down.’

'You can't do that!' Harri and Ryan chimed.

'You'll kill it!' said Mr Davies. 'The Ancient Briton Re-enactment Society will sue if you do! You'll lose your jobs! We'll make sure of it!'

'You might kill my dad too!' Ryan's voice choked as his eyes welled up with tears.

Ryan's mum sighed and put her head in her hands. 'I don't know what we did to deserve all this!'

'Then it's up to you, Harri,' said the Chief Constable. 'If you can't think of anything to stop the dragon, we'll have to call in the army, with guns and rockets and helicopters and all.'

Imelda stepped forward and put her hand on Harri's head. 'I think you need to go and talk with Tân,' she said, softly.

Everyone in the room straightened up. They stared at Harri and spoke with one voice. 'You can talk to dragons?'

Chapter Ten

'Do it now!' Draca growled.

Ryan's dad switched on his new phone. There was only one number stored in its memory. He'd copied it from Ryan's phone.

There was one bar of signal available. Just enough. He wrote his text message, pressed send and switched the phone off. He didn't want to make it too easy to be found just yet.

A trumpet fanfare blew on Harri's phone, letting him know he'd had a message. Harri frowned. The only two people who sent him messages were in the room. Mum occasionally asked him what he wanted for tea or if he could pick something up from the supermarket on the way home from school,

and sometimes Ryan sent a message about homework or maybe a link to a funny YouTube video.

Who else would be trying to contact him?

Each pair of eyes in the room watched as he took the phone out of his pocket and read the message out loud.

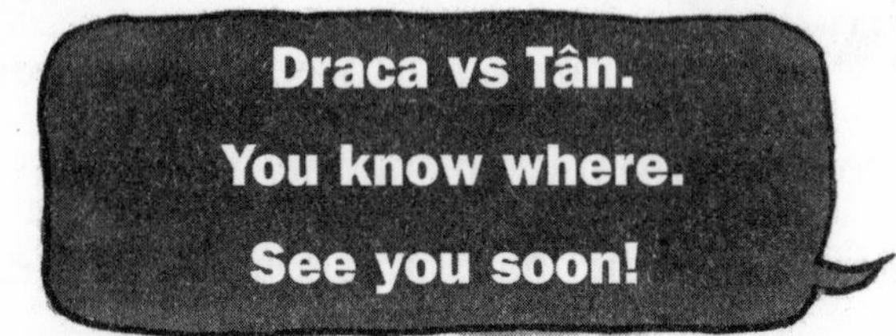

'It's your dad!' Harri told Ryan. 'How'd he get my number?'

Ryan looked confused and guilty. His dad kept getting in the way of his and Harri's friendship. 'He must have copied it off my phone. He's such a…'

'Are you sure it's him?' the Chief Constable interrupted, before Ryan could say anything too bad about his dad.

'I'm certain,' said Harri. 'No one else would think to send that message.'

'He says, "Draca vs Tân, you know where..." Do you know where he means?' asked DS Hughes.

Harri stole a glance at Imelda. She made another one of those tiny movements — a blink and the slightest tilt of her head that was as good as saying, 'Don't tell them, Harri!'

'No!' said Harri, slightly worried that he was getting so good at lying to the police.

'Would Tân know?' the policewoman asked.

'Maybe.'

'Then you'd better go and ask him,' she smiled.

Chapter Eleven

Harri, Ryan, their mums and Imelda were driven to the castle in a police van, escorted by the Chief Constable's car and four police motorcycle outriders. As Tân's chief sponsor, Mr Davies had demanded to come too. The cameramen and reporters crowded round and followed them down the High Street.

'I need to talk to Tân on my own,' Harri explained. 'He'll get nervous with everyone else around.'

He climbed the steps and walked down the long, dark passageway. He could already hear Tân calling excitedly in his head.

He punched in the code to open the heavy iron door of the dragon's lair, went in and sat down on the straw next to Tân, whose tail rattled and

shimmered with the excitement of seeing his master twice in one day.

'I don't know what to do, Tân.' Harri put his arm around Tân's neck.

The dragon's voice rang clear in his head. 'What will be, will be,' Tân said, unhelpfully. 'We have to do what we have to do.'

'But what do we have to do?' Harri felt very frustrated. He wanted answers not riddles!

'I have to face Draca in a fight probably to the death. That is why you and Ryan's dad made us.'

'I never did!' Harri was horrified that Tân could think that. He hadn't planned this. It was Imelda's fault, if anyone was to blame. It was her magic that brought Tân into the world.

'I never meant any of this to happen.' Tears of frustration welled up in Harri's eyes. 'I never thought you would be a real, live dragon.'

'I know,' Tân's voice soothed. 'But once I was

made, a course was set. When Draca was made, the final destination was certain.'

'Final destination? What do you mean? Where? Why?'

'There is only one destination…'

'Dinas Emrys!' Harri whispered.

That place had been calling him since the first day he heard about it in Mr Davies' lesson. Harri thought about what Imelda had said earlier, how Merlin had been a fatherless child. He thought again how he had never met his father, hadn't heard from him for years… How he was a fatherless child.

'Am I Emrys?' Harri asked. 'Am I Merlin?'

'I don't know.' Tân's eyes crinkled into a dragon smile. He seemed to have grown yet again. Harri was still his master, but now it was time for Tân to take charge and look after him. 'We must go to Dinas Emrys to find out and see what will be.'

Chapter Twelve

Ryan's dad took the protective cover off the lens of his digital night-scope and scanned the surrounding countryside. All was quiet. A main road ran through the valley, but no one was driving at this time of night. There were dragons about! The news reports said only to travel if it was absolutely necessary.

In the distance, the wooded slopes of Dinas Emrys rose up from the valley floor. It was a perfect, natural stronghold, an obvious place to build a fortress, so obvious that Ryan's dad knew that they shouldn't base their camp there. That's where *they* would go. That's where *they* would be looking for him.

A fox screamed in the distance.

Bleating lambs called out to their mothers.

'Get some sleep,' Draca growled. 'They'll come

for sure, don't you worry. We'll know it when they do.'

Ryan's dad tucked himself into his goosedown-filled sleeping bag and made himself comfy in the bracken next to Draca.

He watched the stars twinkle overhead. The Milky Way stretched out across the heavens. You had to be outside, in total darkness, to appreciate the beauty of it all. A warm breeze floated across the hillside, smelling sweet and earthy. Soon it would be daylight. Soon it would be the Eve of May Day.

Chapter Thirteen

The alarm on Harri's phone rang for a split second. He pulled it out from under the pillow and silenced it quickly.

5:00 am!

Harri and Tân had planned everything. Being able to talk in your head was great. No one could overhear you or bug you with hidden microphones.

Harri needed to be out of the house before the town woke up.

His clothes lay ready in a neat pile. As he slipped into them, Dylan, his cat, stretched, turned round three times and settled down again on the bed. Harri could start the day early if he wanted to. This was sleeping time for cats.

Harri picked up the backpack he'd got ready the night before and took one last look around the

room in case he'd missed something. Peaking through a gap in the curtains of the landing window, he saw the TV satellite dishes pointing skywards from a string of vans parked out in the street. Japan TV, USA Today, Chinese and Russian TV vans had turned up last night. This story was going worldwide.

Harri gulped from a carton of milk and ate a couple of chocolate digestives from the biscuit tin. Then he unzipped a banana and ate it as he sneaked out of the back door.

Once he'd climbed the wall at the bottom of the garden, he knew all was well. There were no reporters here and he knew all the secret back routes around the town.

Streaks of dawn were spreading slowly in the east, but the hills kept the rising sun well hidden behind them.

Keeping to the murky shadows, he snaked his way through back alleys and quiet, sleeping streets

to the park and the dark side of the castle. No cameras were watching there, where the walls rose up from the shadows, exactly where Ryan's dad had started climbing just over twenty-four hours before.

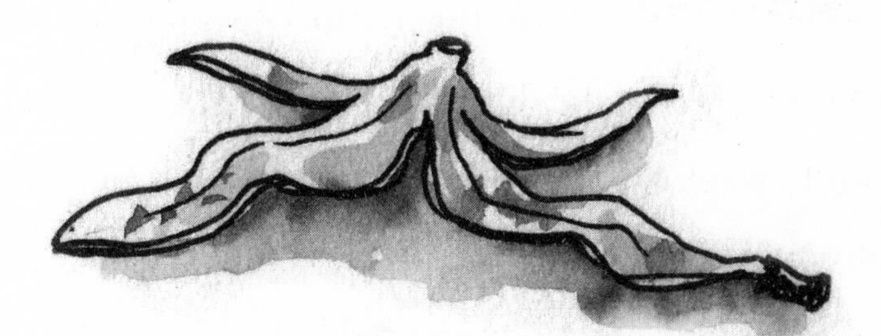

Chapter Fourteen

'He's on the move!' a voice spoke quietly into DS Hughes' headset. The earpiece meant no one could hear the radio conversations or the crackle of static during the silences. DS Hughes didn't want anyone to know that she was out and about at that time of day. 'He should be with you any moment,' the voice assured her.

Secretly, a team of detectives had been set up all around the town. One of them watched and waited in the alley behind the shop. He gave a running commentary of Harri's early morning manoeuvres on his radio.

'I see him,' DS Hughes whispered into her headset. She'd been a policewoman a long time. She'd seen a lot of things and been in a lot of scary situations, so she had learned to stay calm under pressure.

But this was different. Dragons! Nothing in the police rule book told you how to deal with dragons, or boys — or grown men, for that matter — who seemed to have fallen under their spell.

This was probably going to be the biggest case of her police career. Her heart fluttered.

What should she do? Watch and wait. She could hear her boss's words as if he was standing next to her.

DCI Griffiths was her boss but also her teacher. He'd been a detective a long time. Watch and wait, he always told her… Watch and wait.

The boy looked up to the top of the tower, then he reached for a handhold and hauled himself up onto the first block of the massive foundations.

Watch and wait.

If he fell and she hadn't tried to stop him, that would be the end of her career. If she stopped him, then who knew what would happen? Harri was the key to this whole dragon thing. There was already

one dangerous dragon out there, killing sheep and tearing them apart. How long before it started attacking humans?

And what of the human with it? DS Hughes thought Ryan's dad should probably be in a psychiatric hospital. Who knew what he might do next? If only they could have kept him locked up in the police station the day before... Sometimes the law was so clever, it got in the way of doing what was right.

And Harri — what was he keeping from her? He was lying through his teeth when he said he knew nothing, and that his dragon, Tân, knew nothing too. She and DCI Griffiths could spot a liar a mile off, and Harri was a terrible liar. He was just a nice kid who'd found himself in a situation that he couldn't handle.

But he was handling the castle walls pretty well. He was half way up. It would be more dangerous to try and stop him now.

'Come on, lad,' she whispered. 'You can do it!'

'Sorry, Sarge?' a voice crackled in her ear. 'Did you say something?'

DS Hughes smiled, crossed her fingers and watched the boy climb higher and higher.

Chapter Fifteen

The walls of the castle leaned in slightly. Harri had climbed far more difficult rock faces up in the hills behind the town. He and Ryan used to go there to let Tân fly free. It was a wild, empty wilderness. They only ever saw a few dog walkers or the occasional tourist, who paid little attention to a couple of boys playing on the rocks.

Harri couldn't walk past a rock face without wanting to climb to the top, where Tân would meet him, flying circles round him in excitement. One particular rock leaned outwards — the opposite to the tower. It was so hard to climb. Harri always felt he was going to fall off backwards.

But the tower was much higher than anything he'd climbed before. The crumbling mortar created spaces between the granite blocks that made it

almost like climbing a giant ladder. So it wasn't difficult, but it was very high!

Harri sang to himself, a tuneless song whose only words were, 'Don't look down!'

And then, suddenly, he was pulling himself over the parapet and safely onto the roof. He didn't go to church, but he was surprised to find himself saying, 'Thank you, God!'

Harri reached under the metal straps that held the flagpole upright and released a small magnetic box. He slid the lid open and took out the key.

Tod the Plod had shown it to him. Tod used to be a policeman but now he was semi-retired and looked after the security at the castle.

Once, the door to the tower roof had blown shut and Tod had been stuck there for hours, so he'd put a spare key in the magnetic key-box just in case it happened again. He'd shown it to Harri one day, in case he ever got stuck on the roof too.

'But what about burglars?' Harri had asked.

'I don't think any burglar would think to look for a hidden key up here!' Tod had laughed.

And now here was Harri, unlocking the door and creeping down the dark, tiny, spiral stairway. He was allowed into the castle to see Tân anytime. He was allowed in through the front door, but this time he was breaking in. Was he a burglar?

'No! You are a rescuer coming to do what has to be done,' Tân's voice spoke in his head.

'I'm here!' Harri whispered. It was like whispering, but he did it in his head. His lips didn't move and he made no sound.

Tân smiled as their eyes met through the bars.

'How are we going to get you out? If I use my keycard and the code, an alarm goes off somewhere and they'll know I'm here.'

'Hide round the corner,' Tân laughed. 'I'll sort this out.'

Harri pinned himself against the old stone walls and waited.

The rumble in Tân's stomach began quietly, building. Burning, sulphurous smoke drifted down the passageway, irritating the back of Harri's nose.

The rumble grew into a roar. The passage lit up as Tân blew a fine stream of white hot flames at the lock, which melted instantly.

The door swung open and Tân leapt into the passage, free.

An alarm began ringing somewhere and powerful jets of water burst from the sprinklers in the ceiling, drenching them.

'It's the fire alarm!' Harri yelled over the noise. 'I didn't think of that! Quick, follow me up to the roof.'

Tân seemed to have grown even more. He barely fitted through the passageway. It was a tight squeeze following Harri up the old, twisty staircase.

Like Draca the night before, Tân was struck by the wonder of being outside in the fresh air and, like Draca too, he unfurled his wings and blew out the

last remaining jets of flame, extinguishing the fires he had stoked to free himself.

'Wow!' Harri blinked in the heat and flame. 'You could have escaped anytime!'

'I could have,' Tân replied. 'But you didn't want me to. Now things have changed. Come on. Climb on my back. We need to get away while we can.'

Well done, Harri, thought DS Hughes, as the dragon leaped off the side of the castle with Harri clinging on tightly round its neck. You are one plucky lad.

She pressed the switch on her radio and talked into her headset. 'Okay! Operation Firestorm is underway. Do not lose sight of that dragon! I need constant reports of where they are.'

'Roger, Sarge!' A chorus of voices answered in her earpiece.

DS Hughes walked to the baker's shop on the

corner that was just opening up. She bought a couple of bacon rolls and two cups of coffee, one with two sugars and one black without — the way her boss liked it. It was time they met up and planned the rest of the day. They needed to start Operation Firestorm.

Chapter Sixteen

An old lady walked down the street unnoticed. She wore a long, green, velvet cloak held together at the neck with a huge diamond-covered star. Her pointed hat was a little bit crumpled.

Anyone watching her might think it looked like a witch's hat. But no one was watching her. She had a way of making herself *almost* invisible. If you did notice her, you too would see the strange way people looked right past her, as if she wasn't there.

She went past the TV vans, the cameras and lights and the good-looking TV presenters, who were rehearsing their lines, eating bacon rolls and drinking coffee from paper cups.

Two or three quiet streets away, she slipped round the side of a block of flats to a row of

garages, where she unlocked and rolled up one of the doors.

When Imelda came to live with Harri and his mum, she had rented the garage from an old lady who didn't drive and didn't need it anymore.

Imelda started up the little van that she kept for her trips to the countryside, where she collected the herbs and flowers and other plants that she used for her spells and potions.

Harri called her to let her know what he'd done.

She sighed deeply, knowing how much trouble lay ahead, but she tried to reassure him. 'You have to do what you have to do, Harri. Can you remember the wood where I took you in the summer? The place where the oak trees opened up into that grassy circle? I'll meet you there so you can tell me your plan. Now switch off your phone. The police can use it to track your movements, you know?'

At the other end of the line, Harri stared at his

phone in horror. He held down the side button and swiped the phone off. He never knew they could do that with your phone!

'Damn!' DS Hughes was watching the google map when Harri's pin symbol disappeared. 'He's switched his phone off — who was he calling?'

The detective who was monitoring Harri's phone called across the busy operations room. 'He was calling an Imelda Spelltravers.… Is that any help?'

'That's the old lady that lives with them,' said the DS. 'Check she's still there.'

DS Hughes had detectives watching the front and the back of the shop and a woman constable inside. She'd been with Harri's mum since she'd broken the news to her of Harri's early morning escapade.

All three radioed that no one had entered or left the shop.

'I think we need to go and see Imelda Spelltravers,' said the DCI. 'She knows much more than she's letting on.'

The constable looked very uncomfortable when they arrived. She hadn't seen Imelda leave the shop. She'd just disappeared!

Harri's mum looked confused. 'I think Imelda went out a little while ago,' she said.

'Are you sure?' asked DCI Griffiths. 'Could we just check?'

Harri's mum slumped in a kitchen chair. 'Of course you can look around, but I'm sure she went out.' The constable raised her eyebrows and scratched her head in confusion. It was a mystery!

'There's a lot of weird stuff in this shop, boss,' said DS Hughes, picking up a box of dried frogs.

'Well, it is a magic shop,' said the DCI. 'I don't think there's a law against any of it. Look, see, everything has proper safety labels on it.'

'Can you inform us as soon as Mrs Spelltravers

returns?' DS Hughes asked Harri's mum. 'And if Harri comes home too.'

Outside, DS Hughes slammed the car door shut. She was baffled. 'How did the old girl get out of the house without being noticed, Boss?'

DCI Griffiths shrugged. 'Magic?' he suggested.

A voice crackled on the radio. 'She's got a van.'

'I want everyone out looking for it!' the DCI ordered into the microphone.

Slowly and clearly, the voice repeated the registration number over the police radio network.

'What do we do now?' DS Hughes asked.

'We watch and wait,' said the DCI with a resigned smile. 'We watch and wait.'

Chapter Seventeen

'The dragons of old always fought on the eve of May Day,' Imelda reminded Harri. 'Tomorrow is the first of May so today is the Eve of May Day.'

They had met up in the oak wood. It was a long way off the beaten track. The little road leading up to it had grass growing down the middle. No one ever used it. The grass swished at the underside of her van as she rattled along the uneven surface and parked by an old, wooden wicket gate.

The oak trees surrounded an oval clearing. The trees had been planted many hundreds of years ago by the druids. It was a special, magical place where rare plants and herbs grew. Harri and Tân were waiting for her, enjoying the warm, spring sun that shone down on the flower-strewn meadow.

Bumblebees droned lazily from buttercups to clover.

'He wants to meet us at Dinas Emrys,' Harri said, nervously.

'Then that's where you must go.' Imelda held Harri's gaze. 'Here, I brought you some food. You should hide here for the rest of the day. No one will ever find you here, this place is not on any map.'

She handed Harri a bottle of brown liquid. 'Drink this at sunset, before you fly to Dinas Emrys. It will

give you strength and keep you wide awake.' She reached out and touched the dragon gently on the cheek. 'After that, it's all up to you, Tân.'

Tân growled his appreciation.

'Good luck, you two,' she said, starting up the van. 'I'll see you when I see you.'

If Harri had not had Tân with him, he would have felt very small, very scared and all alone in the world.

Chapter Eighteen

Ryan's dad watched the sun sink down behind the mountains. A feeling of excitement grew inside him. Draca's greed and hunger for treasure had infected him. It was spreading through his mind and body like a virus or a cancer. Merlin's treasure was just across the valley. He could feel the power of it calling them. He could almost touch it.

Draca snored and snuffled, sleeping off the sheep he'd killed and eaten the day before. Draca had acquired a huge appetite for blood and fresh meat. Now and then he growled and twitched as he fought imaginary enemies in his dreams.

Police helicopters had been looking for them, flying around the mountains all day, but they were hidden under an overhanging rock. No one would

ever find them there and their heat-seeking cameras couldn't see through two metres of rock.

He switched on his phone and sent a brief message.

Chapter Nineteen

'I want to see the detective in charge of the dragon case, please.' Mr Davies leaned assertively on the reception counter at the police station. Being a schoolteacher gave him a sense of being in command. He was dressed as the leader of the Ancient Briton Re-enactment Society, or the Red Dragons, as they liked to be called.

A group of hairy, bearded warriors squeezed into the small waiting room with him. More warriors, including members of the Ancient Saxons, who were old friends as well as weekend enemies, milled around outside, clunking their shields, rattling their swords and waving battleaxes in the air.

'Can I help?' DCI Griffiths' voice cut through the hubbub, making the rowdy crowd hush.

'We know where the battle will be!' Mr Davies

gushed. 'We've worked it out, see? It's all there in the *Mabinogion* and the *Historia Brittonum*!' Mr Davies held up copies of the ancient books.

'I'm sorry?' The DCI smiled patiently, as he would to a four-year-old child. 'What battle? And *Historia* what?'

'Tomorrow is May Day,' Mr Davies explained. 'The red and the white dragon of old fought every year on the eve of May Day. They were captured and buried at Dinas Emrys. Years later they escaped. Now they're alive again, they must return to Dinas Emrys for the Final Battle.'

'Ho! The Final Battle!' chorused the bearded warriors, stamping the floor and pounding the air with their fists.

'Well, thank you for the tip off,' said DCI Griffiths. 'We'll add that to our information database.'

Back in the control room of Operation Firestorm, the DCI sighed heavily. 'Please tell me they are a bunch of fruitcakes, Beth!' he said to DS Hughes.

She wrinkled her nose. 'Sometimes it's the fruitcakes that solve the cases,' she laughed. 'Where is this Dinas Emrys, anyway?'

She typed the name into Google and a map popped up.

'It's a rocky, wooded hillock near Beddgelert on the A498,' she read aloud. 'Yes,' she confirmed. 'There's a whole lot of stuff written here about dragons too.'

'Imelda's van has just been spotted!' a detective called across the room.

'How did she get out of that shop without anyone seeing her?' DS Hughes suspected her detectives had been sleeping while watching the shop.

'Where was the van sighted?' asked the DCI.

The detective consulted his screen, 'Err … Beddgelert on the A498,' he announced.

The DS and the DCI gave each other a look as if to say, 'Now, that's a coincidence!' But to the police, there is no such thing as a coincidence.

Chapter Twenty

'It's time, Harri,' said Tân. 'The sun is going down. We must be on our way.'

A chill ran through the boy's body. His legs trembled and his hands shook. This was it. How had he ever ended up in a magic oak wood, about to join battle with his best friend's dad and an angry, bad-tempered dragon?

He fished in his back pocket and brought out DS Hughes' business card. He stared at it in the darkening gloom and remembered what she had said.

'That's my phone number. If you get any ideas or remember anything or need help, call me any time, day or night… Promise?' She'd made him promise and he had.

He was just a boy with a dragon. Maybe he

should warn the policewoman and let her know what was about to happen.

He pulled out his phone and switched it on. One bar. The signal was weak here. It blew a fanfare as it registered with the network. Harri nearly dropped it. A message. From *him*!

This situation was too big for him, but he didn't want to speak to DS Hughes. He knew she'd keep him talking, and try to get him to give himself up. Give himself up? He really sounded like a criminal now! And what about Tân? The law that had protected him was now out looking for him. Tân was a fugitive from justice — and most likely Harri was too!

DS Hughes was a detective. All she really needed was a clue.

Harri typed his message, pressed send and switched the phone off. The liquid in the bottle that Imelda had given him tasted like peaches. It tasted much better than it looked.

He stood, stretched, put on his backpack and zipped up his jacket. 'Come on, Tân,' he said in a firm, strong voice. 'Let's go!'

Chapter Twenty-one

DS Hughes' phone pinged. It pinged all day with messages, but something made her check this one immediately. The tension was high in the operations room. Everyone knew that something big was about to happen, but no one knew what or where.

That name again — too much coincidence. She double checked the number. Harri!

She stood up so quickly her wheeled chair shot across the office floor. She grabbed her coat and shouted over the hubbub. 'Get everyone together and get everything we have to Dinas Emrys on the A498 near Beddgelert. GO!'

All the detectives and uniformed police officers in the room sprang into action, picking up keys, coats and bags, phoning colleagues and finishing off the dregs in their coffee cups.

'Will we need the firearms unit?' someone called.

'Yes!' DS Hughes ordered. 'And the dogs! And get the helicopter up in the air!'

Outside the police station, Mr Davies had been holding council with his men. Now they had come to a decision.

Mr Davies climbed up onto the wall. A sea of hairy, bearded faces stared up at him, waiting for their orders.

'Men!' he bellowed, thrusting a deadly-looking axe in the air. 'Tonight is the Eve of May Day. Our dragons will meet at Dinas Emrys and we should be there with them!'

The hairy, bearded warriors murmured their agreement.

'Are you ready, men?'

The hairy, bearded warriors raised spears, swords and axes.

As one, they cheered, 'To Dinas Emrys!'

The hairy, bearded warriors piled into minivans and Land Rovers, whooping and chanting their songs of war.

Chapter Twenty-two

Imelda saw them first. She leaned against an ash tree in the Grove of the Magicians. It was ancient, protected ground, so it would be a safe place for her to watch the battle unfold. She kneaded a ball of beeswax in her hand, making it soft enough to mould and block her ears up. The sound was going to be terrible.

A moment later, Ryan's dad saw them too, a tiny dot in the distance. He watched them fly down the valley with the long, slow, sweeping beat of Tân's wings. Was Tân bigger than he remembered? He was such a puny little thing the last time he'd looked in Tân's castle lair and sneered. Draca was a true, fighting dragon, he'd made sure

of that when he had planned and drawn him for Imelda to bring to life, but he'd always thought of Tân as just a little pet. Now he wasn't so sure. A sliver of doubt entered his mind. Maybe this wasn't going to be such an easy fight after all?

'We shall win,' Draca growled, reading his thoughts.

Tân circled Dynas Emrys. Was it a hill or a mound? It was big and rocky but it could never be called a mountain.

'Down there!' Harri pointed to a place where the wooded canopy opened up and bare rock faced the hillside. 'I remember that place from when we came before. I think you should put me down there.'

'It is the entrance to Merlin's Cave,' Tân said, banking steeply and spiralling down to the spot Harri had pointed to. His sharp claws reached out and grasped hold of the rocky crags as they landed in the small clearing.

It didn't look like a cave. It was just a huge wall of rock. He couldn't see any holes or cracks. There was no way in. 'What happens now?' Harri asked.

Tân looked up. An inky, liquid shape glided across the night sky creating a ripple in the starlight. Harri was surprised how well he could see in the dark. Was that Imelda's potion at work?

Draca landed gracefully on the summit of the hill.

'Well, Dragling?' he sneered, in a rough, booming voice that Harri heard as clearly as if Tân were speaking. 'Are you ready?'

Tân turned to Harri. 'Always remember that none of this is of your doing. You just happened to be the right child at the right place at the right time.'

Harri flung his arms around the dragon's scaly neck. Tears rolled from his eyes. Were they really going to fight to the death?

There was nothing more to say.

'Stay here,' said Tân. 'You have your part to play.' His head rose high and his chest puffed out bravely and proudly as he glowered at his foe. His unfurled wings rattled in the gentle breeze.

'Bye, Harri. Stay safe.'

Rolling over the edge of the rock, the leathery skin of his wings snapped tight as the wind caught his fall. Tân glided silently over the treetops and into the darkness.

Where was he? What was his plan? Harri scrunched his eyes up and stared into the night. He could see amazingly well, but there was no sign of Tân. Poor Harri! There was nothing he could do.

Chapter Twenty-three

Tân knew that surprise was his best tactic. Warm air was still rising from the road, which had heated up in the sun during the day. Tân felt himself lifted on the rising thermal. He let it take him high above Dinas Emrys.

Far below, Harri was a tiny dot and Draca was a fat, lazy, but very dangerous dragon, stalking the top of the hill, waiting for battle to begin.

'Come on, Dragling!' Draca roared into the night. 'I'm waiting!'

Tân rolled off the column of warm air, tucked his wings into his sides and fell like a brick. Within metres of Draca, his wings cracked open, braking his fall. His talons lashed out, tearing a hole in Draca's wing. Draca screamed with rage. Sparks flew out of his nostrils. His wings spread wide as he took off into the night.

Dragon fires can be lit by anger or by choice. Either way, dragons can only keep their fires burning for so long. Tân spun a cartwheel in the air, so he could make a sharp turn. Sweeping in behind Draca again, he lashed at the steel-hard scales on his back.

Draca roared again. Curling tongues of flame streamed out of his mouth and nostrils. His fires were alight, just as Tân had hoped. If he could keep those fires burning, Draca would lose strength and his most fearful weapon … fire!

Sparks and sputtering flames left a smoky trail in the air. In the darkness, there was nowhere for Draca to hide. Tân attacked again and again, lashing out with his vicious claws. But Draca's skin was hard as nails. The only places to cause him real damage were his soft undersides or a killer bite to the throat. That would be a dangerous move. Tân would have to tire Draca first.

Draca may have been a bit slow from eating too many sheep, but he was not stupid. He dropped to

the ground and hid among the trees while he calmed the fires within, banking the sparks and cinders for when he would really need them later.

A glowing arc of moonlight rose up behind the mountains that surrounded them. Tân stood proud, a dragon silhouette atop a craggy pinnacle, watching … waiting for signs of the next attack.

In the Grove of the Magicians, a rhyme from an ancient book spun round and round Imelda's head.

'Full Moon on Mayday Eve,
Dragon fire will mountains cleve.'

'This is it!' she whispered into the night.

Chapter Twenty-four

The giant, yellow circle of the moon rose into the sky, casting silver light and hard shadows across the valley. To Harri it was as good as daylight. 'Behind you, Tân!' he screamed, as Draca dropped out of the sky.

Neither dragon could hide now, they were both plainly visible. Their dragon scales caught the moonlight, refracting and reflecting it so they almost glowed, one white, one red, streaking across the starry heavens.

Now it was a battle to the end. They swooped and plunged, glittering claws spraying showers of sparks, as they slammed into each other's flinty, scaly skin.

Screaming, roaring, bellowing, howling with rage, anger, courage and pain, they came back at

each other time and time again. With each clash, showers of broken scales floated through the air, catching the moonlight in a twinkling, hazy mist.

As their armour weakened, so the blows became more painful and the bellowing shrieks grew even louder. Nothing moved in the valley. Sheep, foxes, mice, owls and insects all fell silent, cowering in fear, hiding wherever they could find shelter. In his lair, Ryan's dad howled in pain. He wore expensive ear defenders, but they were no match for the deafening screams from above.

Again and again the dragons crashed into each other until, high above Dinas Emrys, their wings shredded and almost incapable of holding them aloft, they grappled and fell.

Above them, the whup-whup-whup of the police helicopter added to the din. A dazzling, bright light burst out of the sky, a shining column of power.

Too tired and battle-damaged to fly any more, the dragons faced each other on the hilltop. In the

helicopter's searchlight, they were clearly visible, like actors on a stage or gladiators in an arena.

They hurled themselves at each other, their jaws opened wide, their dagger-like teeth aimed at each other's throats. They fought and writhed, their long, snake-like bodies twisting, curling, coiling around each other as they tried desperately to force a killer blow.

Down below, Harri seemed protected from the noise. Maybe that was Imelda's potion at work again? He heard Tân's voice in his head, not talking but grunting and groaning, as he gave as good as he got.

Far down the valley, flashing blue lights and a cacophony of sirens joined the sound and fury of the fray. Then came the roar of their engines, thrashing through the gears, whining at top speed. Another ribbon of vehicles snaked up the valley from the other direction, braking, screeching, sliding across the road, headlights shooting off in wild, crazy directions.

'What the…!' Harri couldn't believe his eyes. Mr Davies and The Ancient Britons and Saxons poured out of their vehicles. Waving burning torches, they charged up the wooded hillside.

'This is the police!' announced a voice from the sky. 'Go back to your vehicles. Your lives are in danger!'

Mr Davies' bearded, hairy warriors took no heed. Their blood was up. There was no more re-enactment for them — this was the real thing!

On top of Dinas Emrys, the warriors made a semicircle around the dragons. A hundred flickering flames glittered in the dragon's eyes. For a moment, they stopped fighting and stared at the little army that surrounded them.

Draca chuckled. His belly trembled, then with a boom like thunder, a sheet of flame blasted towards the men. Realising just how real this was, the warriors broke ranks and ran for cover. Draca tossed his head back and roared with joy. 'Stupid men!'

Draca's fires and anger were alight. There was no stopping him now.

'Open the cave!' Tân's voice filled Harri's head.

'How?' Harri called back?

'Just do it!' Tân ordered.

Chapter Twenty-five

Harri stood in front of the rock face. He felt so stupid. All around him, lights and engines, voices and dragon screams confused him. Tân's voice filled his head. 'Just do it!'

But how? Across the valley he saw a movement. A man, well camouflaged but picked out by the moon's hard shadow, was running through the bracken towards the road. Ryan's dad! Harri had almost forgotten about him. This was all his fault — but never mind that now!

Harri turned to the wall of rock and shook his head. How do you do magic? How do you open solid rock?

'Open sesame?' he said, hesitantly. It was all he could think of. Nothing happened.

'You have to do better than that!' Tân's voice filled

his head. 'Be forceful! Take command! You are the fatherless child! Tonight you are Emrys!'

That phrase 'fatherless child' at once made him feel so alone and yet it made him feel powerful too. There was only him now, there was no one else to count on for help. Being a fatherless child made him feel responsible — in charge of his own destiny.

He drew himself up to his full height and ignored the tumult around him.

Once again, Imelda's words returned to him.

'Emrys is the old Welsh name for Merlin. They say that the chamber under Dinas Emrys is still full of Merlin's gold and that one day a fatherless child will come to claim it. A bell will ring and the mountain will open for him.'

The hairs on Harri's neck stood up on end and his arms prickled with gooseflesh. A phrase that he had heard again and again in the last few days, came to him. He placed the palm of his hand firmly against the rock and called in a clear, firm voice of authority.

'What will be, will be!'

A single, resounding strike of an enormous bell rang out, shaking the mountainside and the roots of the trees that clung to the thin rocky ground. The sound reverberated down the valley like a tidal wave, knocking anyone who stood in its path to the ground.

The earth beneath Harri's feet began to quake. A tiny, hairline crack appeared in the rock beneath his hand. Dirt and pebbles fell from above as the crack grew wider and wider still. The rock was moving! Splitting in two, heaving itself with a deep, dry, dusty, grinding groan. Two doors slid in opposite directions, melting into the side of the hill.

Harri took out his phone, turned on the light and held it above his head. The bright electronic beam revealed the entrance to a vast underground chamber. A huge stone trough filled the centre, its lid lying broken on the floor.

‘King Lludd’s stone coffer!’ Harri whispered in awe. Then he saw the treasure. Harri’s finger tapped the camera icon on the screen of his phone.

The screen lit up. Gold, silver, pearls, rubies, emeralds and diamonds glinted and twinkled. It looked like those illustrations of pirate treasure or Ali Baba’s cave from the picture books Mum used to read to him. He pressed the record button.

His moment of peace was shattered. The bright, starlit entrance darkened as Tân, with wings in tatters, skidded through the rocky portal into Merlin’s chamber.

Draca crashed into the cave right behind him. As he gained his balance, his hungry, yellow eyes opened wide in astonishment. His pupils shrank into narrow slits, taking in the brilliance of the sparkling jewels and gleaming gold.

There is nothing a greedy dragon loves more than gold and precious stones, and Draca was filled to bursting with greed and desire for gold. Ryan’s

dad had made him that way from the start. He had drawn him like that. For a moment Draca was dazzled. His eyes glowed as he took in the sight. He wanted to own it all, to bury his face in this shining, sparkling treasure.

Only one thing was in his way.

Draca had Tân cornered. There was no escape.

Only this silly red dragon stood in his way. He would soon put an end to him.

Like a coiled spring, Draca unleashed himself at Tân, claws flashing, eyes wide and wild with hatred and loathing, teeth bared, slavering with foaming spit. Tân fought bravely, snarling, slashing at Draca's soft throat.

'Tân!' Harri yelled. 'Watch out!'

Draca paused. Silence flooded the chamber. Slowly, his head turned to face Harri, pinning the boy with a cold, heartless stare. Draca's thin, transparent inner lids slid over the slits of his eyes as he breathed in a long, slow, relentless breath. His

chest and stomach filled, his shoulders raised and his neck arched as if preparing himself for a great onslaught. The rumbling in his belly began to build in volume, the vibrations filling the chamber, rattling the gold plates and goblets, making strings of pearls dance like luminous snakes.

'Run!' Tân's voice bellowed in Harri's head. Tân leaped in front of Draca, protecting Harri from the fires that were building up inside the deadly creature.

Harri hesitated.

'Run and close the mountain behind you!'

Draca paused, realising that he was about to be trapped inside the cave forever. Again, he turned his huge, scaly head towards Harri. He fixed him with a look of venom and hatred and took in an enormous breath, understanding it was now or never.

'Run! NOW!' Tân's voice filled Harri's head with panic.

Harri ran, tripping, stumbling, hurling himself at the entrance. He saw that Tân fought hard to protect him as he ran for safety. Draca's fires erupted like a volcano. He saw the flames that chased after him only as glittering reflections in the shining precious metals, as he hurled himself at the entrance.

As he crossed the threshold and breathed fresh air, a man appeared in front of him. Ryan's dad! His head snapped back in a maniacal cry. 'I win!' he laughed like a drunken, wild hyena.

The ball of flame roared up the passage from the treasure chamber.

Harri couldn't think of any magic words to say. 'Close the chamber doors!' he yelled, throwing himself sideways, rugby-tackling Ryan's dad to the ground with him.

The earth shook once again, as the giant slabs of rock slid out of the hillside. Draca's last blast of flame poured out of the entrance. Ryan's dad's glasses lit up, reflecting the dazzling, chemical colours, as the inferno rolled over them.

The doors to the hillside crashed together. The thin crack between them disappeared as if someone had erased it from the top to the bottom.

Silence descended. The helicopter light shone down on Harri and that was the last thing he remembered.

Chapter Twenty-six

Harri had a room of his own at the hospital.

He wasn't really hurt, but they wanted to keep an eye on him just in case he had concussion or something worse.

They came and went: Mum, the police…

The police had so many questions. They had no idea what to say or what to do. The dragons were locked up in the hillside. No one was badly hurt. No laws seemed to have been broken.

The National Trust people were a bit upset about the mess, but pleased that Dinas Emrys was in the national news.

Imelda stayed at his bedside, just in case hospital medicine wasn't enough. Just in case he might need her and the old ways. She sat by his bedside, knitting quietly — almost invisible —

watching the comings and goings, protecting her precious charge.

Ryan and his mum popped in. They were visiting Ryan's dad, who was in another room at the end of the ward. Ryan's mum brought him a huge basket of fruit and a pile of comics.

'It's such a shame about Tân,' said Ryan. 'Do you think he's dead? And Draca too? I hope so, I hated that dragon.'

'Ryan!' Ryan's mum tapped him on the elbow. 'What a thing to say to poor Harri!'

Harri fiddled with the corner of a comic.

Ryan did his best to cheer up his friend. 'I loved it when we went flying Tân up in the hills,' he said. 'Maybe you should get a dog instead?'

Harri smiled, 'I don't think our cat would like that!'

Mr Davies and his men had been told to go home and cool off! He was not allowed to visit Harri. Harri needed rest. He would have to wait until Harri

was well enough to go back to school to get the full story.

Harri wasn't hurt, but he was so tired. He was half watching a wildlife film on the TV. Humpback whales leaped out of the ocean, twisting, turning and crashing back into the water. The singing whale's soundtrack made him feel sleepy. Imelda's knitting needles click-clacked quietly in the corner.

A knock, and the door cracked open.

'Mr Mitchell!'

Ryan's dad poked his head into the room.

'Can I come in?' He was in a hospital dressing gown. A bandage covered his head. Another was wrapped around his right hand, which poked out of a sling. His face was covered in small cuts and grazes and his right eye was puffy and blackened with bruising.

'Are you okay?' Harri scrabbled to sit up.

'Just a few cuts and bruises,' he laughed and

shrugged his shoulders. He struggled to hold Harri's gaze, then stared down at his slippers.

The TV programme droned on, filling the awkward silence.

'I... ' Ryan's dad hesitated.

Harri waited.

'I... I just wanted to say sorry.'

Their eyes met. They both knew what he meant and that he truly meant it. Only Harri could ever understand or forgive him.

'It's like Draca was made from a part of me ... like he was made out of the bad side of me.' Nervously, he looked across at Imelda, who pursed her lips, nodded, raised an eyebrow and carried on knitting.

'Now Draca's gone I feel different. I can remember the greed and the longing for gold and treasure and that we would both do anything to get it, but now Draca is gone, all that has gone from me too.'

'Good.' Harri smiled and nodded. 'I understand.'

Ryan's dad held his hand out. Harri took it and shook it gently — a sign of friendship and forgiveness between one dragon-master and another.

'Thank you, Harri.'

Ryan's dad made a little bow in Imelda's direction and gently closed the door behind him.

Harri slumped down into the deep, soft pillow.

'If he's free of Draca's spell,' Imelda asked, 'is Draca really dead and gone?'

Harri reached for his phone, swiped it on and pressed play. He'd watched the video many times already and would watch it many times more.

The flaming jets poured from Draca's throat. Gold and silver shone brightly in the blaze. Rubies and diamonds glittered as Tân and Draca disappeared behind the roaring inferno. Flames filled the screen, rolling towards the camera. Dark shapes slid in from either side of the screen as the chamber door met in the middle, locking the dragons away … for ever? The video kept recording as the camera fell to the ground. It focussed on some pebbles and a small spider that was creeping out of harm's way.

'I think so,' Harri sighed.

Drowsily, Harri pressed the play button again. As he watched, Tân's last words came back into his head, just as they had done at Dinas Emrys. Tân's last words, that had filled his head as the rocky mountainside crashed shut, locking the two dragons inside, alone with Merlin's gold.

'Run for your life, Harri!' Tân's voice had reverberated round his brain. 'Don't worry about me – this is where the legend ends. We dragons are safe here. We'll sleep until we're needed. Run and I'll see you again, Harri, when both you and the time are ready. Now, RUN!'

And he had run, almost sure that Tân was right and that they would meet again one day.

Harri's eyelids drooped shut. The hypnotic clicking of Imelda's needles sent him drifting into a long, exhausted sleep.

Harri's lips moved as he smiled in his sleep. Imelda leaned forward, straining to hear what he was saying.

'I'll see you again, Harri, when both you and the time are ready.'